Then they skated off to have hot chocolate with marshmallows and talk about snowflakes.

"How does it look?" he asked, joining her on the hill.
"I've never seen anything like it before!" cried Viola. "What is it?"
"It looks like a big scribble to me," snickered Otto.
"It's a snowflake," said Dozer. "Can't you tell?"
"Of course I can!" sighed Viola.

The crowd cheered Dozer. "OOOOOH!"
Swine! thought Otto.
"You are the winner," said Viola. "*No one* can do what you can do."
Otto said, "Well, you *are* different!"
"Watch me skate some more," said Dozer.

When he was done, Viola could see a shape traced in the ice.

When he did, Dozer saw the shapes that he had traced in the ice. He was amazed. They were not perfectly round circles or straight lines, but stars, trees, cars, lightbulbs, and even a piano.

"Wow!" cried Dozer.

"Oh my, you may not be able to do a bunny hop, but you are an artist on skates!" said Viola.

Dozer stopped and called out, "Oh Viola, I guess I didn't really believe I was a snowflake."

"Dozer, turn around and look!" cried Viola.

Viola was very upset. "What's wrong with that elephant!" she grumbled.
"He forgot everything I taught him. He's just a bumbling lump."
Viola climbed the hill for a snack while Dozer continued to skitter on the ice.
Otto was on the hill laughing with his friends.

All eyes turned to Dozer. He tripped over the laces of his skates—*Plunk!*—and fell on his rear end. His bunny hop flopped and he skated around and around, never making a circle. Everyone laughed.

"Dozer can't skate! HA! HA!" they giggled over and over again.

Otto went first. He hopped very high and spun around and around in perfect circles. He raced backward and lifted one skate gracefully toward the sky.

Otto was on the ice very early the next morning. He practiced his bunny hops and spins. He zigzagged and raced very fast.

Dozer and Viola watched Otto from the edge of the pond.

Otto jumped and twirled by them. He made a face at Dozer.

"I think I want to go home now," said Dozer.

"If you remember everything I told you, you will be great," said Viola.

"I hope so," said Dozer.

Viola called Dozer on the telephone. "I hope you remember to dream about perfect circles and bunny hops," said Viola.

"I don't feel so good," said Dozer.
Dozer hung up the phone and lay down. He tried to sleep but he just felt too nervous. He wondered how it would feel to be as light as a feather and as graceful as a swan. All he felt was clunky and scared.

After supper Dozer sat in his bedroom and looked at the moon outside his window.

Maybe the ice will melt on the pond, thought Dozer.

"I made believe I was skating on a cloud," said Dozer looking up at her, "and my toes got stuck in the ice. If I make believe I'm a snowflake, I might fall *through* the ice."

Dozer got to his feet.

"That's it," he said. "I am going home now. Maybe Otto will forget to come here tomorrow," said Dozer.

"He won't forget," said Viola. "Everyone from school will be here. But if you dream about being a great skater tonight, you will skate perfectly tomorrow."

Dozer tried to jump, but his toes got stuck in the ice. He tottered for a moment, swinging his arms. And then…*Boooom!*…he crashed into Viola.

Ice flew in all directions as Dozer tried to hop like a bunny. Instead he landed with a thud, just like an elephant. He traced very wobbly circles and spun around on his rear end.

"Nuts!" said Dozer.

"Oh, Dozer," Viola sighed. "If you make believe that you are as light as a snowflake," she said, "you will be."

Viola twirled around first on her right foot and then on her left. She hopped like
a bunny and spun like a top, and each time she jumped she landed gracefully.

"Now you try it, Dozer," Viola said. "Keep your ankles steady, your toes even,
and bend your knees. Make believe you are skating on a cloud."

"This ice is slippery," said Dozer. "I can't get up."

"All ice is slippery," said Viola as she helped him. "I never fall because I am as light as a feather and as graceful as a swan. Watch me."

After school Viola waited for Dozer at the pond. The ice was filled with skaters. Viola was so busy watching them, she did not see Dozer moving gingerly across the ice. But she sure noticed him when he fell at her feet.

In the classroom Otto whispered to his friends. They looked at Dozer and snickered.

"They are laughing already," Dozer said to Viola. "What will I do?"

"Meet me at the pond after school," said Viola. "I'll show you how to skate like me."

"I won a blue ribbon in skating last year," said Otto. "Can you spin on one skate?"

"Yes," said Dozer.

"Can you skate in a perfect circle?" asked Otto.

"Of course," mumbled Dozer.

"Meet me tomorrow at the pond," said Otto. "We will see who is the better skater."

"Okay," whispered Dozer.

When Otto had gone, Viola looked at Dozer and sighed. "Now you are in big trouble," she said. "Everyone is going to laugh at you. You can't skate."

Dozer's feelings were hurt, but he got to his feet, mustered up his courage, and said, "When I skate, I am never clumsy and I never fall down. I am the best ice skater in Pruneville."

Everyone laughed.

Dozer slid onto the pond and knocked over Otto. Otto was the biggest kid in the class.

Now I've done it, thought Dozer as he lay on the ice looking up at king-size Otto.

"Dozer, you're such a blunderhead," said Viola.

"That's why we don't let you play hockey with us," boomed Otto.

Dozer got back on his sled and zoomed toward the pond in the school yard. From the top of the hill he could see his friend Viola.

"Viola!" he called.

"You're ten minutes late!" she trumpeted.

Dozer was getting closer to the pond. He tried to stop his sled, but it hit a piece of ice and just kept on going.

"Gangway! I can't stop!" cried Dozer.

"Look out!" Viola exclaimed.

"Watch where you're going!" hollered the cheese man. The huge yellow wheels rolled down the street and knocked over two elderly ladies.

"It was an accident," Dozer said as he helped them up.

The sled hit a big bump on the sidewalk and Dozer zipped along faster than he had ever zipped before. The sidewalk ahead was clear.

Suddenly a deliveryman carrying three huge wheels of smelly Swiss cheese opened the door of his truck and stepped onto the sidewalk.

"No brakes!" shouted Dozer. *Crash!*

"Look out!" shouted Dozer, but it was too late. Mr. Broom and the holiday cards and letters flew up into the air and landed in the snow.

"Dozer, that's the third time this week you have knocked me down. Everyone's mail is soggy," yelled Mr. Broom.

"Sorry," Dozer said, but he could not stop. Faster...faster...the sled whizzed down the hill.

"Oh no!" cried Dozer. The sled raced out of control, made a sharp right turn past Mrs. Hogg's prickly thornbush, and...*Oooops!*...sailed into Mr. Broom who was about to put a letter in the mailbox.

"Dozer! Hurry up or you'll be late for school," yelled his mother.

One breezy Friday morning Dozer jumped on his sled to school. The air was icy
cold and every time he let out a breath, Dozer could see thick fog drifting out of his
long nose. At the end of his street the sled hit a large patch of ice.

— For Richard —

Published by Dial Books for Young Readers
A Division of Penguin Books USA Inc.
375 Hudson Street
New York, New York 10014

Design by Mara Nussbaum
Printed in Hong Kong by
South China Printing Company (1988) Limited
First Edition
1 3 5 7 9 10 8 6 4 2

Library of Congress Cataloging in Publication Data
DiVito, Anna.
Elephants on ice / by Anna DiVito.
p.   cm.
Summary: When a clumsy elephant named Dozer
is challenged to an ice skating contest by his schoolmate Otto,
he wins in an unexpected way.
ISBN 0-8037-0797-5 (trade)—ISBN 0-8037-0798-3 (library)
[1. Elephants—Fiction. 2. Ice skating—Fiction.] I. Title.
PZ7.D635E1 1991 [E]—dc20 90-22392 CIP AC

The art for each picture consists of an ink-and-watercolor
painting, which is scanner-separated and reproduced
in full color.

ELEPHANTS ON ICE

STORY AND PICTURES BY **Anna DiVito**

DIAL BOOKS FOR YOUNG READERS *New York*